To the Other Side

Story by Kathryn Sutherland

Illustrations by Lisa Simmons

Contents

Chapter I

Refugees

You might expect a busload of people heading off to start a new life to be a noisy, buzzing crowd, but on this journey, barely a word was spoken. There was coughing because of the thick, smoky air, but nobody talked. Some people slept on this journey of many hours. They were the lucky ones — for fear, regret, and sadness prevented sleep in most.

Anna simply stared out the bus window in silence.

The smoky haze prevented Anna from seeing anything clearly, but occasional fireballs lit the sky and she could make out a few remaining familiar landmarks in the distance. Tears rolled down her cheeks. Mom hugged her and rocked her, for her own comfort as much as Anna's.

The bus chugged with great effort up the mountain road — a narrow trail, not used to the heavy traffic of recent weeks. It was barely wide enough for a bus, and certainly not wide enough for oncoming vehicles to pass. Thankfully, none were traveling in the opposite direction. Nobody was entering Anna's troubled homeland. People were leaving in droves.

As their steep climb progressed, the scenery became less and less familiar. The trees were different. There were very few houses around. Eventually the air became clean and the coughing reduced in frequency. When darkness fell, Anna slept a little.

She awoke with a start at the border. Guards boarded the bus and shined flashlights in their faces.

"Any documents?" they were asking in a language she didn't understand. "Passports?"

Anna's mom showed a guard what they had.

"No visas?" he asked.

Mom shook her head apologetically, guessing what he was saying.

"No passport for the girl?"

Again Mom shook her head. Anna felt Mom's grip around her shoulders tighten. A pain shot down the arm she'd injured in the fall from her tree. That seemed like a long time ago now. She looked across at Dad and the others.

The guard frowned. He called a colleague over and showed him the documents. They mumbled to each other and looked at the other passengers, then mumbled some more.

"What if they don't let us in?" Anna asked.

Mom shrugged, too nervous to answer. But the second guard took charge and smiled at them. "Refugees," he said. "Okay."

Everyone on the bus was a refugee, escaping the war. The guards herded them off the bus and into a cold, tin shed. "Wait here," they said.

★ ★ ★

They waited a long time in the mountain shed, shivering in the chilly night air. Anna's family huddled close together: Anna, Mom, Dad, Uncle Malek, Aunt Jana, baby Lena, and Grandpa, who was coughing again. Anna wrapped her scarf around him. With most of her wardrobe on, she had plenty to spare.

"What's happening? What are we waiting for?" asked Anna.

"We're waiting for another bus," said Dad, "to take us to a refugee camp."

Anna's eyes brightened. "A camp? We're going camping? Oh, great, some good luck at last! I loved our last camping trip."

"This won't be quite the same," Dad replied, "but it will be an adventure, Anna."

A guard returned. "There is room on the bus for three people only. The baby should go. It's too cold here."

"But there are seven of us," said Uncle Malek.

"There is room for three people only," the guard repeated.

"You go," said Dad to Malek and his family. "Another bus will come for us. We'll catch up at the camp, I'm sure."

Chapter 2

The Camp

The passengers relaxed on the bus trip from the border to the camp. Most people managed to sleep, though many chose to chatter.

"I wonder how long we'll be at the camp?"

"What will the accommodations be like?"

As dawn broke, the refugee camp came into view. Anna's jaw dropped at the sight. Tents stretched on forever: row after row of huge, green army tents — nothing like the little tent Anna's family took camping.

"You were right, Dad," said Anna, bitterly. "This will be nothing like our camping trip. This is a tent city."

"It'll be fine, love," Dad replied. "We'll be safe here, and there will be plenty of kids here, too. You'll make new friends."

The passengers began collecting their few belongings together as the bus slowed to a halt. A young man with a friendly smile stepped onto the bus and said "Good morning" and "Welcome" in Anna's language. All the passengers answered his greeting and began firing questions at him. But he didn't answer. "Good morning" and "Welcome" was all he knew. He shrugged, smiled again, and gestured for everyone to sit down.

Moments later, a young woman stepped onto the bus. "Good morning, I'm Dana Alic. This is Greg Mills, a camp supervisor. The staff at this camp speak English, so I shall be your interpreter. Please listen carefully."

Greg continued, "I welcome you here and am glad you arrived safely. I hope your journey was not too difficult."

Dana translated his words exactly, so all the passengers could understand.

"Please wait patiently while we assign you a tent." Greg looked through a folder, then said, "Tent F13 can take four more. Is there a family of four here?"

Dana translated, and Dad's hand shot up.

"Fine. Give me your names, then a volunteer will show you to tent F13."

Each row of tents had a sign. As they passed each "street," the volunteer named them in English: A, B, C, D, E . . .

Mom and Anna repeated each in turn.

He turned at Row F.

"F," they repeated.

He counted the numbers as they passed each tent.

"I can't learn these numbers!" said Anna.

"Just learn our tent's number," said Mom, despairingly. "13 . . . Tent F13."

Chapter 3

Tent City

There were 16 other people living in tent F13. Anna balked at the idea of sharing with strangers, especially 16 of them! She had found her own house too noisy — even before Uncle Malek and his family had to move in when their own house was bombed. But when Dad did the introductions, she forced a smile.

"I hope you don't mind us moving in with you," Mom said to the occupants. There was no reply, just stares and an awkward silence.

"Let's take a look around the camp, Anna," Mom continued. "Are you two coming?" she asked Dad and Grandpa.

Grandpa shook his head. He lay down on his cot and put his earpiece in to listen to his old transistor radio.

"I'll come," said Dad. "Let's find out where Malek and the others are." Dad seemed more cheerful here than at home. "At least we don't have to share a tent with Malek's baby!"

"I miss baby Lena," Anna replied, sadly.

The administration tent was easy to find. It was the only tent that wasn't green. Dana helped them look through the computer listing of camp residents, but there was no record of Uncle Malek and his family. "I'm sorry, they must be in another refugee camp. There are four in this area."

Dad was optimistic. "We'll trace them."

"Now, let's get you organized," Dana continued. "Here's a map of the camp. You can collect food from the shed opposite here every week. Here's your ration card. Your time for collection is Friday at 1:15 P.M. There's also a school in the tent next to the playground."

"Do I have to go?" Anna hadn't thought about school in ages.

"No, but it's a good way to make new friends, and you can learn English and German," Dana explained.

"Why?" Anna asked.

"You don't know where you'll go from here, so it's good to prepare for different countries."

"No, we'll go home soon!" said Anna.

Mom frowned at Anna's rude tone. Dad put his hand on Anna's arm. "Let's continue our tour. Thanks, Dana."

"Here's the toilet block," said Mom. "I'll just pop in. Coming, Anna?"

Anna followed, but ran straight back out, holding her nose. "Ugh! Gross!"

A girl about her age walked past and laughed. "The toilets take a bit of getting used to . . . 18,000 people and no sewers."

"I'm never going back in there!" exclaimed Anna.

"You'll have to go some time!" replied the girl, still laughing.

Anna waited for Mom on the grass, sitting with her head slumped. This was all too horrible.

Chapter 4

Dad's Search

Dad was determined to trace Uncle Malek and his family. He wrote letters to all the camps and checked each day at the administration tent for a reply. He wrote letters to everyone he knew, seeking information. He even sent letters to offices in the war zone asking if there was any news of Malek.

Week after week he did this, without losing hope.

Chapter 5

Eva

One Friday, Mom returned from the ration shed with a young girl. Anna recognized her from the toilet block that first day. "Anna, this is Eva. I've invited her for dinner."

"Hi, Eva," said Anna flatly.

Eva was more sociable. "I'm glad your arm is better, Anna. No sling anymore!"

Dinner was meager: bread, canned meat, and potatoes. Eva brought some biscuits. She was sweet and very chatty. Anna knew Eva had been invited to try and cheer her up. Mom was tired of Anna's whining. Annoyed, Anna tried not to be friendly to Eva, but found herself laughing at Eva's jokes in no time.

"Come to school with me, Anna," Eva encouraged. "I'll pick you up in the morning."

Anna nodded. Mom and Dad smiled. They'd tried for weeks to get Anna to go to school, but she'd refused.

Classes were more casual than at Anna's old school — lots of art and discussions about war, plus music, math, German, and English.

"I don't need to learn English or German," Anna repeated stubbornly. "I'm going home when the war ends."

"Hmm. Maybe." The teacher patted her shoulder. "Back to your work."

"What did you do at school?" Mom asked.

Anna said nothing, but handed over a crushed piece of paper.

Running away from our troubled homeland

Everyone has seen too much horror and sadness

Fear of pain, fear of death

Unknown future

Get help for my country and all of us in it

Eighteen thousand people in this freezing tent city

Everyone aching to go home

Conditions are bad: crowded and unhealthy

Always hungry, bored, and homesick

Maybe we should have stayed in the war zone

Please help me get out of here

Anna, 11

"Poor darling . . . I'll talk to Dad." Mom gently brushed back the hair flopping down over Anna's eyes. "Now, paste this poem in your sketchbook. And then, why don't you sketch a few sights of the camp?"

"I don't feel like drawing here." Anna lay back on her cot and shut out all the noises of the camp. But in the distance she could hear the continuing bombing of her homeland. It sent shivers down her spine.

Finally, after a few weeks, Anna took her sketchbook to school. Some classmates recognized places she'd drawn and shared their memories.

"My grandparents lived there!" one said.

"We used to have picnics in that park!" said another.

Anna told them about shows at the theater, dance classes at City Hall, and life on the quiet hillside above the city. A tear fell when she showed them the twig of leaves she'd kept from the tree where she did her sketching.

"I could see right across the valley from up in my thinking tree. My uncle called these leaves 'Anna's eyes'," she reminisced. "The tree burned down with my house."

"One day you can go back and plant a new tree, Anna," said Eva. "Look, there are seed pods on the twig."

Anna's eyes lit up. Her new friend had given her hope.

Chapter 6

The Search Is Over

Three months after they'd arrived, Dad finally received a letter. "Malek! They're okay."

Mom sighed with relief. Anna jumped around squealing. "Where are they?"

"In America."

Anna stopped jumping. "America! That's on the other side of the world!"

Grandpa seemed to age ten years at that moment. "I'll never see them again," he said.

Mom sat silent, looking confused. Then she grabbed the letter and read it aloud.

Anna listened intently. After all Uncle Malek, Aunt Jana, and baby Lena had been through, it made sense for them to go far away.

Anna understood, but tears dribbled down her cheeks anyway. "I'm going to find Eva."

Mom and Dad were deep in discussion when she returned. Grandpa had his earphones on, refusing to take part. He was coughing.

"Sit up more, Grandpa." Anna helped him up and his breathing eased a little.

"Anna, what would you say to joining Malek and the others in America?" Dad asked.

"NO! I want to go home."

"Honey, we can't. Grandpa heard on the radio that the city has been devastated and the hillside is taken over by snipers. They're not letting anyone return. Anyway, I couldn't bear seeing the destruction."

"We have to go back, Dad!" cried Anna.

"Mom and I want to make a new start somewhere. We've seen enough sadness," said Dad.

"We can make a new start at home. We can fix the house," Anna implored.

"No, Anna. Let's join Malek in America," replied Dad.

Anna ran out of the tent sobbing, off to tell her woes to Eva. Oh, no, what about Eva? She couldn't leave Eva.

"Don't worry," said Eva. "It'll take forever for the paperwork to be processed, and they probably won't accept you anyway. My mom's been trying to get us into Germany for six months, with no luck. And do you think America would want a crazy person like you, who's terrified of toilets!"

Anna hugged Eva. She always made Anna feel better.

★ ★ ★

But within a month everything was arranged. With only a few meager belongings, packing could wait until the morning of their departure.

It was then that Grandpa made his announcement. "I am too old to travel so far. I want to die in my own country."

He was not going with them.

Chapter 7

To the Other Side

Anna, Mom, and Dad stopped still. They stared at Grandpa, shocked.

"But our country is destroyed!" Dad argued. "It will be years before it is safe again."

"I will wait." Grandpa would not change his mind.

"Then we'll stay, too," said Anna.

"No. You are young. You can make a new life in a new country. I can see that's best for you and your parents."

"We don't have to go," Mom told him. "We can't leave you here alone."

"Alone?" Grandpa laughed. "I'm with thousands of my people. I am not alone. No, you go. I'll stay."

Anna was worried. Grandpa was ill. Would he make it home? She dreaded the thought of him dying here, alone in a foreign country.

But Grandpa had timed his announcement cunningly, and Anna secretly shared his wishes.

"I'll come home to visit you as soon as I can, Grandpa," said Anna. Impulsively, she opened her sketchbook. She handed Grandpa the twig of leaves she'd brought from home, from her thinking tree that had been destroyed.

"Anna's eyes!" said Grandpa. "That's what Uncle Malek called these leaves, didn't he?"

Anna was crying as she nodded. "Look, there's a seed pod on it. I thought you could plant it when you get home. One day, I'll come back and see it . . . when it's growing . . ."

Grandpa hugged Anna tightly.

Eva came to say goodbye. "I'll look after him," she said, through tears. "I need a grandpa." Then she smiled. "Write to me in English — if you ever learn it!"

"I wish I'd paid more attention in school. If you didn't talk so much, I might have," said Anna, and she squeezed Eva's hand tightly.

Anna and her parents boarded the bus. As the bus pulled away, Anna held the gaze of Grandpa and Eva, until they became tiny specks in the distance. Then, finally, she turned her attention to the journey ahead of her. Another bus trip, another new destination.